The Dailiness

*For Lia —*

# The Dailiness

## Lauren Camp

*Lauren Camp*
*Teatro Paraguas*
*Feb. 2014*

Printed in the United States of America
First edition: December 2013
ISBN 978-1-6192755-6-0


Grateful acknowledgment is made for permission to reprint the
selection from *A Musical Hell* by Alejandra Pizarnik, copyright
©1971 by Alejandra Pizarnik, 2000, 2013 by Myriam Pizarnik de
Nesis, Translation copyright 2013 by Yvette Siegert. Reprinted by
permission of New Directions Publishing Corp.


Cover photo by Lauren Camp • laurencamp.com
Author photo by Elena E. Giorgi

Published by Edwin E. Smith Publishing • edwinesmith.com
199 Clark Road, McRae, Arkansas 72102

*To the scar of memory. To Lynn Mukamal, my mother.*

*And to David, again.*

# Contents

——————————————————————— **Three**

"—The flower of distance is blooming. I want you to look through the window and tell me what you see: inconclusive gestures, illusory objects, failed shapes... Go to the window as if you'd been preparing for this your entire life."

Alejandra Pizarnik

# One

## Looking Around These Days

Tiny ants began appearing in my kitchen last week. The same day,
the market closed down 200 points, the thermometer outside
the window reached 98 and everyone's humor came unsutured.

Men behind freeways collided with bent bodies,
lengthening the list of things they needed toward the magnetic field
of the moon. Dogs began their daily barking.

In Albuquerque, a man devoted his existence to anxiety. He argued
in his sleep, begging for exoneration from foreclosure and insolvency.
His wife's eyes staggered about. A family of quail hobbled past.

That day, a doctor lost four patients in the stitched light of ending,
and I ate small ants with dinner.

Downtown, a man drifted off in a martini sleep, glimpsing
random riddles of his creator as if the world mattered only
in shades of skewered olive. He waited for a phone to ring.

And a man with pistachios in his blood sold energy down every street,
reminding himself that he was not a failure.
He tallied doors and locks as justice.

Ants stamped small feet forward, then gathered in black whorls.
In Hollywood, a woman in a kingdom of children knitted
one hundred white sweaters.

The day moved forward with six dropped purls of tension
and a small furrow of calories. In her overheated bedroom,
the woman's face tightened.

Somewhere, a man perched on the side of his body going in and out
of fear. Each room of thought draped with cancer. To the hospital,
people sent pink cards of chance,

In the south, on the glass beach where repentance was again missing,
turtles dropped their eggs slowly. The ants keep reappearing.
To keep the kitchen clean, we wipe, then drown them.

## November

This is a lopsided world when your smile
reminds me of things that have been discarded.

Everything you see now is pretend:
nine sad syllables of uncertainty.

If we start at the end,
perhaps you will forget the day I threw rocks,

every tooth of exhaustion
ripped out, every road lined in pine. If there was a night,

I would have slept. Instead, I walked for a year,
my center buried in routes I kept passing.

## Rail Runner Express Crash on 1-25
## South of Santa Fe

One summer day, I witnessed the murder
of speed and money, a train
and armored car twined beneath a pockmarked sun.

I missed the tire squeal, but sat
in the nervous framework of vehicles
that bloomed down the Interstate. An ambulance

had been dispatched. We all gawked
as an EMT tended the scrapes and whispers
flung against the road — in this same threadbare spot

where a gasoline truck toppled, then exploded
several months before, metal
melting to its unsuspecting driver.

Even now I fear the whack, the severed bodies
swallowing thready air.

How much easier it is to be looking over
what has rolled over through light fragmented
on the underside of someone else's car.

We continue driving forward, frantically strategizing
details and errands until we meet tomorrow's headline.

But this is my bend in the road,
my wrecked railing.

A personality test defines me as lemon-sour
so I take the test again, changing answers.

Forgive me.

This time it calls me blue
and I become a river of blue, flowing back and forth
on the Interstate in my beat-up Subaru,

never putting my compassion down,
never leaving the road with my imperfect eyes.

## Toward Summer

Riding a bike up the hill
toward summer, I enter
a vast field of understanding.
My wheels carve tracks
through the rapid language
of morning. Shifting gears,
I unfurl past a woman
reading backward
from a long book of myths,
its spine boundless, unlaced.
I can tell the story is unfolding
because tiny words and letters
drop in piles as she turns pages.
A strange code of bold
and swerved italics litter the grass.
Verbs and adjectives trickle
down, punctuating the plain
with puddles of serifs and dashes.
Indents and spaces evaporate.
I keep pedaling, powered
by a white light blazing
off the pages where text once
ordered itself into prepositions
and clauses. A pocket-
sized corona moves in and out,
tumbling over the woman
extracting meaning from
a book dropping answers.
In this meadow where she sits,
light drips down her arms.
Light without name and
light without burden.
Getting down from my bike,
I gather armfuls of words,
portable paragraphs of thought,
and return them to the woman
who smiles, then tells me
of her life from the ending first,
spinning out sentences
in slow revolutions.

# Drama Class, 1989

No set or costume, no one else on stage,
just the thin sound of my tongue uttering
a long sheet of Tillie Olsen's weary words.

It was the wrong choice, this monologue.
I had not yet pressed my life into creases
or folds, hadn't even a small furrow of pain.

In class, my soft hands sprawled along
an invisible board, ironing abstract air.

I groped for next lines, my right arm floating
in an eccentric display of space.

Steadfast on the script, my light voice
draped with youth. The iron zigged
and scorched, then nosed up. Poor Mrs. E,

the drama teacher, who pressed on me
to let exhaustion settle in, to let it steam
from Tillie's worn dark story.

*Slowly!* she warned, all stiff and calicoed.
*Iron as you do at home. Concentrate.*
*Be particular about the sleeves and seams.*

But I had never shaped a shirt, never
laundered a mistake, didn't know to poke
toward sags and puckers, how to wait.

That fake iron couldn't straighten any life.
I needed time to bend and smooth
some dangers, to snag and mess again.

Back then my life was long, unrolled —
everything flat, still frivolous, unwrinkled.

## Time

Clocks always argue for and against.
Halfway fast — or folded behind.

When you say no, I murmur back
in whispers. We leave short arguments

on the floor for later. I manage the house.
Or can't manage.

9 o'clock unfolds but time exaggerates
into a cup of tea and clover flowers.

A short talk on what's real
while I pet the missing cat.

Not touching makes us vulnerable

to constellations of red,
so we paint the kitchen. Knives gather

without jackets.
The landscape is spectacle and serrated.

Outside, three dogs carousing, a tent of juniper,
an inverted hourglass of light.

## Unpacked

The red car stayed red until I was 30. I moved away
too late in search of flaming hills,
carried your words
like a satchel on a long journey.
I tasted adventure's grease and color,
the wicked span of globe.

Unpacking was never easy.
Something always left behind
until the part that looks like you was all I had left.

Once a tepid girl in a corner, a mass of tangled
hair and thoughts —
you knew me then. The world was bound
in shelves around our house. Sun glimmered slowly,
yellow as dried nettles
— and I grew,
moldy and without promise.

## Girl on a Bus

While her folks covered the full distance
of an argument, she entered the station at 2nd

and Main; at the counter, she scheduled
the nervous destination of Hope

because she believed
it might exist. The girl was raised sharp,

spent after-school hours on a rickety bicycle
and climbed fences to tangle with freedom.

She never ratted on the bargain business
conducted in alleys, never minded

the dark steam of each day lifting
from the flat table of tar,

but she's tired of her parents' wrinkled moods;
that's why she's traveling

through a sepia rendering of tomorrow
on a bus faltering along.

Almost noon,
and Hope is the flat middle of the country.

The polyester seat gums into her shorts,
then pops when she leans forward.

The girl's eyes are rivet and handle
on a porous childhood:

the kind that doesn't often matter.
This yellow bus rearranged her future,

and now she thinks
she's getting somewhere. She traces

the journey on her leg, then pinches her skin
to put in a mountain, to climb over something

other than her heart. In the bus,
she almost feels buoyant.

## And Now You Would

And now you would know how she folded
each part of her body into a small blue space

and that she is counting
the twelve days left

And next you would know that she was robbed
of all her secrets and stood stammering

and unable to fasten her house in the wind
and the seats would be wet again

And you would have told her *no*
and that she was indolent
that she must not apologize to anyone

and she would remain in bed
where you would hear her sing lazy to the moon
all the obsolete meanings and questions

of yesterday
and the plane would arrive and land
in a single room of her mind

And you would know that she had been waiting
and she would see through a square hole
for more than a week

her eyes active but her heart rested
and next you would know she is lying

yet her words are a hurricane
you want to be in the middle of

for one more day at least
and the point is rising

And you will not understand the language
but are willing to be carried backward
into the space before sense

where sound rolls sideways in your mouth

## For Those of You

For those of you who were there, my mother was a wizard,
sharp as a chicken bone that night, diagramming the long passage
through the room with each of our normal names. Two hundred
and four hands holding knives and forks, and her daughter
about to write a strange history of love on a stolen book

crinkled with hope. I was thin that day, my body golden.
For those of you who were there, the night was flannel; my mother
was careful about spelling, flushed and warm. Our faces
were her fiction, her tongue flowering with what was written
on her eyes. In minutes she wove us into words,

her voice twined with wine. If you were there, you know
she was meticulous in her memory, name-wedging unmarried men
between yards of ancient relatives after the post-pork posole
heartburn and the damnedest red chile in Albuquerque,
her databank rapidly outputting inventory into a lengthy list

of scattered people. For those of you who don't know,
my understanding of connection is clamped to that night
of elongated peace some years before she died, when she tallied
the wild folds of each of us in one long expository list, the night
she indexed all of us into a galaxy of necessary stars.

## Ten Years

where did you day and day gone
and you in the cement the blossoms the wind

approaching a flawless illusion I decide to live
with intention there needs to be someone to hear

what causes pain the threads undoing I am tired
of the effort (not mad) the sun still

out but dimmer some days scratched
transparent unseeing the dry anger of loss ravishing

at night I taste bare words on my tongue
unravel into a discussion with myself

each point of memory in ten years
you must have changed into shadow or light

you are everything I remake
every day you were only borrowed

what does your voice sound like we are missing
our days full of shade do you

hear me from the distance of your new home the nest
of clouds my mouth asks for you remember that

## My Grandfather and His Eggs

My Papa raised the flattened sun on a Tulsa sky
each weekday morning. Tall and hollow,

he was suspended in a life sunny side up.
9 to 5, he candled eggs, sorted them by color

then headed home to boiled eggs. Papa played piano.
He carried his lungs in a shirt pocket, his humor

in a highball glass. Sometimes Papa painted portraits;
his life was drawn in charcoal.

Papa steeped his eggs in oleo. Papa fried his fears.
On weekends, Papa walked nine holes of golf

then sank into his armchair. Papa lit a cigarette.
Papa by TV,  Papa with his glasses.

My mom was fragile when he died.
We watched her eyes go runny,

how she slid into the pan
of what was missing.

I tell you grief can lay eggs anywhere.
Pale and delicate, Mom dreamt her daddy

in the bowl of heaven.
She saw Papa in her photos, heard Papa

in her whispers. Papa drinking gin,
Papa over easy. Now Mom has moved

through that same membrane, and without her,
life in our house keeps breaking open.

## Even If

Even if the sun is tall and everything is only gently burning,
put all the grief from your mother's cancer in your front pocket.

There is no wind now, just your losses.
When the dark is still hungry, give it an ankle, a broken bone.

Give it saliva and feces —
the exactness of what is cruel.

You have brought almost nothing with you
but what you own cannot be taken back.

These memories make up the line you must hold,
an invisible ridge, the inky dark.

Even if they are wet or unmarked, this is only
the waking moment. Bring back your mother's soup,

her square thick glasses. Turn your head into the shifting days
and gulp. Bring that too — the song of yourself swallowing.

## Let Me Live in Your Tolerance

Do not say *salaam aleikum* in my taxi.
Say *Hello*.
Say *Drive me to 42nd and 2nd*.

As we move slowly up the Avenue,
do not ask my faith, and do not ask me if I fast.

What I put in my body nourishes me;
what I leave out also feeds my soul.

Do not get out your knife.
My skin knows its angles already.

Say *Here's your money, sir*
then please remove your soft body from my cab.

---

*[A] baby-faced college student was charged Wednesday with using a folding knife to slash the neck and face of the taxi's Bangladeshi driver after the driver said he was Muslim.*

— *Associated Press / August 26, 2010*

## Dream Pantoum

On the road down, seven times
The musk of skin is salty.
When the balm of existing becomes night,
We move into a thousand endurances.

The musk of skin is salty.
Solid-eyed ghosts in the same bed.
We move into a thousand endurances
Of the bone and muscle of evanescence.

Solid-eyed ghosts in the same bed
Lying always on their most oblique sides
Of the bone and muscle of evanescence
Fit predictions to the tiny sock of your mind.

Lying always on their most oblique sides,
They dress in triple layers of cloud,
Fit predictions to the tiny sock of your mind,
The fleet-footed night, the cuff of life.

They dress in triple layers of cloud
When the balm of existing becomes night.
The fleet-footed night, the cuff of life:
On the road down, seven times.

# In Provincetown

It is easy to be overlooked, easy
to suffer the salt-drunk beauty of a tired
town, the tides of private laughter.

I am here to see the water,
to hear a sea gone mad
with endless moistured breath.

Every day, one hour later than the day
before, I tend the sea, study the same sand.
Low tide is when the music comes:

the call of terns at war for territory,
curve of wind across the open,
talking stripes of light,

sucking sound of rubber boot
on saturated shore,
dug-up slurp of quahogs from sand.

At dusk, I pass through,
hear brown men sing,
hold their mysteries in paper bags.

*Angels*, the pretty boys,
flutter at the east side coffee shop,
men with hair so calligraphed,

so jeweled gold. Narrow bodies,
short skirts, quick drags on hookah pipes,
a faint swell of gentle coughs.

By night, I see rain through the screen,
corrosive anxious heavens,
then open the door to hear inside the water.

Interred in a floated house,
a captain's six-room cottage,
wind reduced to howls, repeating waves

of slamming sound, I have been quiet
weeks, in conversation only
with the fossils on a beach.

# What You Might Hear

*"...when I realized I could make mistakes... I decided I was really on to something."*     — Ornette Coleman

You can tell by the rumble of tall incantations
that he has secured sound into a model of mingling
symbols and masterful spells.

                           Listen for the riddle
inverted in rhythm, and you will want answers. If you
want answers, you must haul the questions behind you
for a long time until the music starts up again, faulty
and brooding.

                           If what you hear
                  slips suddenly into symmetry,
remember that silence travels sideways, that it is
careless and quirky, an omission of space.

The jangle and wriggle are courtly, laughing and lisping
rhetorical notes as he rambles, rapidly changing
timing to truth.

His horn, that pliable prophet of conduct, offers its
sequence of agony, exodus,
               the fanatical fancy of finding devotion.

                     If you cannot respond,
                 he has proven his point,
the rate of the measure, his sounds wrenched in error.
Where he got them won't matter.

If the beat turns colors, it will also get louder,
lumber forward, limp and leap. If you look closely,
you will see his orange heart like a moon.

                     He may offer a cure
             contradiction
       paradox
         a possible
            furious anthem.

        If he offers you meaning, accept.

## Thelonious Monk On A Subway

I met Monk
        on a subway, coming through the tunnel.
            His words fell out be-
tween thick beard hairs,
            then lumbered toward me, paused and sighed.

                When the train jerked, his long
                        fingers reached out,
            touched my pale shoulder:
                    he wore a rust brown coat.


                Intervals rode
the track with us: E flat, D,
            C and D. Harmonious fifths and mismatched chords.

He explained that the melodies
                were dots
        his hands wanted to connect.

                    I didn't understand
            so he invited me to his home.
We emerged from underground and
            walked. Step, step, stop

            over thin tones of San Juan Hill. The sun moved closer.
Step, pause,

step. He smiled
            that slow spreading smile,
                    shook hands with a man
        he knew, mumbled
            and moved on.

                    Step, step.

        On West 63rd, he found his door,
            removed his hat
               and knocked.

Nellie took his hat, and Monk sat.

His fingers lipped
white keys, unlocked black ones.
                                    He tapped,
crossed and banged again,
                    rolled his ring into place.

Evolving patterns
                un-
            clenched in a dance of abrupt
                            imagination, endless extrusion.
                        Music didn't pour out,
        didn't puddle.
He wrung it
from his palms, revived it, gathered it in again and

                        played for hours —
                "'Round Midnight" and "Blue Monk," the angles
        of lines
                merging
until my head was full of squares
                                and curves,
                    the truth of spheres.


He drew silence on that piano
                            in his kitchen
                    until the sun came up.

        I drank another cup of tea
        and left through a small door
                            to the city, the gray-
                green emerging light
        the same as any other day, but


the corners of his melodies
                            kept opening and closing,

            making infinite space
in the chunky dankness of the swilled avenue.

## Value + Pauses

He arrives
wrapped in
a day bag
holding a lock
+ a box
on a wide
bus from Ninth
Avenue / the sky be-
comes musk +
thunder un-
folding / he has
shaved
his head / smokes
a few words per
sentence
expelling old
acorns + city dust /
he's come for
money / running
into the law / the low
ends of his eyes
almost flap
the floor / she sees the
small chart of numbers
he clenches
to challenge his
failure / she turns
as he catches a bus
home two days
on / one
bitten hand
in his pocket
holds insult
the other the fluff
of confusion / rain
knocks on
the window / tells
figures + columns
but he is
laced tight
into darkness

## Philadelphia

Late afternoons,
the small sun slips downtown
past spirituals standing
rag-tied and braided
on street corners.

Immersed in this paste-
and-water city, I watch the moon
rise blindly
across the bridge. Each time
it lifts its large eye,
the rivers huddle.

Brick houses mirror
their images. Dark red façades
swim drunkenly, drenched.

In each pane of jittery glass,
a curve of white. Right now,
this is everything
I can manage.

I read the black clock
across the way.
Its hands never once appear.

Even here,
tomorrow is always tomorrow.

## The *uh-huh* of Desire

The way his hyphen flattened the beveled air,
how it slipped between them
and spread off his tongue
with one of 26 dialects she didn't yet know.

It was this she wanted and this she'd recall:
the edge coming toward her
and the breath
as he paused in that dash,
the sudden architecture of line.

She waited for a story to be written,
and to travel through it, through
the increasing tightened space,
both syllables poised, but resisting.

And she knew she would look back
at that sliver of air,
that original moment of suspension
hung lightly between words,
the moment before persuasion was final.

The subtext of each scarcely moving sound
brimmed over the edge,
and the span of words passed into them
with such economy, such need.

# Two

# Clarity

Either we're standing in disordered light before the disappointment, or it's after, the night bluing and we can't see our hollow habits. We are surrounded by warnings, watch the leaves in the ditch, sun cascading through the eye of a speckled sky. In the absolute, every moment can go wrong. One of us has wings; one looks east at pieces of a city. The air exerts a long wave of wheat. You laugh, and I hear it in my chest. Something about the unspannable relaxes us. The pauses are rarer now, and sometimes we forget to reach for them. To crawl into night takes courage at a frequency we cannot see. Your hair is blowing, curling. We are cold in a backyard stained green from last year's harvest. Our shadows stretch up walls, so we linger, then move over a leach field to a sharp edge where the moon settled. It isn't far, a few cattle guards. The view becomes clear, but also flat. Why can't it be like this all the time, the full earth drawn in transparent layers? We could start to believe in ghosts out here. When we lose our way, we agree to swallow the thorny frost. You notice every detail of dirt, the mournful edges of a grave and next to that, a grave. I see black dots on our white pictures as we enter the blush of trees. And now, a wet spring, a pond, a tangled tent. Raspberries already plump. Red rising in our mouths.

## Out walking

as I have each night this week
— 20 minutes to dusk

it's coming on summer
chamisa not yet in flower but the heat rising 84 degrees

the beginning of night fueled by last moments of day

time is calmer
fringed with heat and the first wordless promise
of breeze

the sun still pricks my skin but the mountain stands by
ready to catch it

and now I understand how you can tell me *stage 4 inoperable cancer*
without choking on fear

because dark will come on as it does

every night


so let it

# The Dailiness

*"...you cup your hands / And gulp from them the dailiness of life."*

*— Randall Jarrell*

*Taos, May 2011*
An arc of dusk climbs the back of twilight. We watch
a spliced horizon.

*Across from Ft. Burgwin*
K focuses his binoculars on a cloud. Night pours by
                in orbit.

*June 4, 2:12 PM*
"Tea or grass," she asks when I arrive: twisted, tense.
            Welcome to share leaves from her drawer.

*Hyde Park, New Mexico foothills*
We hunt paths down the mountain. Spread streets with tires.
            Drive until sun drapes on clouds.

*Marfa, TX*
Through holes, the dense drone of light.
All intersections and space. Boxes.

*Northern New Mexico, Tuesday, August 9, 2011, 3:31 PM*
I hide from stitches of sun — dry and long.
Our mountain continues standing still.

*October 8, La Cienega bedroom*
Yesterday I didn't tell you no.
                I opened wider in the dusk.

*Whole Foods, October 8*
A woman
keeps sticking her hands in the bulk bin: all crystal ginger.

# A Colloquy on Water

We have brought you to the desert,
seven thousand feet above the sea, where the bare ground
seams itself to the unyielding sky.
You are in a region with its own definition of surface tension.
We ask you to understand that the earth is shallow here, unsweetened,
a thin veneer of sediment and below that, knotted clay.
This ground is voracious, but clogged. We do what we can.
We are a people of anticipated guilt: each seed, a mouth,
each flower, a confession. We collect each bead of water
like beggars after coins, and dole out our sum
on the few green corners of our land.
We are efficient and thorough; we chart each tree,
chart the chewable sounds of rain, our ears cunning
and satisfied when each drop, each small volume of liquid,
resonates on the metal roof, then gathers in the gutters,
and funnels down through dry grooves around our home.
We talk endlessly about prisms of sun on the land,
the dry air and wind. We discuss these things in the morning
and again when we pour coffee and make bread.
It is here that you learn about water, not in grottoes and ponds
or snow-glossed trails. This tangled earth, this withering.
Look here, where the wild olive lives, the berried sumac,
this earth, its tart face waiting, the crabapple weeping,
the honey locust, black currant, purple ash, the amurs
and cottonwoods standing, stiffening;
it is here that we draw maps from clouded dishwater
and the fertile remains of each shower,
the puddle of liquid we collect when we wash clothes.
In this place, where we constantly rescue water.

## When You Leave, Reiterate the Alarm
*(New Mexico, June 2011)*

The earth is burning

and I am hiding down our hill, beyond a culvert
and through cottonwood roots.

The wild zigzag of leaves.

Suffocating gape
of sky. I could be anyone

watching satin red birds fly
through the mirror of knowing,
carting their single suitcase to the birdbath.

I breathe the leftover tang of Wallow dust:
eighty-two percent contained.

I breathe Conchas ash blown from the west,
then south by east.

44,000 acres.
Smoke, the way we tone down desert colors.
The only sound the honking arc of ravens.

I sit in this swing rocking back and forth,
dry air cradled between my scissoring legs.

I press my face into the skin of dirt,
rest my cheek on clumps of cool ground,
pray for clouds to leak rain,

a mountain of rain.

## Everything Human
*(for Flip)*

An instant in a yellow hat in the rain.
Half a voice, a whole voice, a bowl of green chile.

Counting our clocks is pointless.

The sky oscillates with neurons of forest fire.

Three weeks. Smoke
draws a steady column from the mountain.

Each speck a disaster,
the enzyme-fixed juice of conclusions,
a margin of pain. Continuous endings.

It hasn't happened yet, but soon

you'll be smaller,
more vapor. Diffuse.

I'll find you in a bed, or on the wooden slats of your porch.

By the branches, the picnic table, the mud.
You can't go far. The other side.

You're on your way past Percocet
through a seminar of love in a trance of sense.

Even time has a background.

You gather sounds, a fresco of jazz. You only have now
to combine a mix of enchantment.

Then you will occupy your musical world.
Wherever you are, you'll listen.

That long structure of tones:

beginning
to end.
And caught in the middle.

# At Echo Canyon
## (Abiquiu, New Mexico)

Slick rock     lost rock
sun on rock and piled rock
dominant rock   sediment rock   bedding rock
million year lithospheric sculpture of rock
firepit of rock
and us sitting in the curve of rock
each word bouncing against rock
a crooked rock trespassing through chasm of rock
the grand earth geologic process of rock
sorted into ambiguous rock
we keep placing our secrets in rock
rock cascade   painted rock
transcendent rock   smart rock   thick rock   solid rock
neighborly rock   the last open rock
salt rock   haunted rock
civilized rock   outcropped rock
rock cove   rough-skinned rock
and knobby knobby motionless
sun-scoured rock
drunken convoluted rock   suffering rock
slipped rock   tender rock   baby rock
stuck rock
plain rock   broken rock
untamed rock   rock rushed from an old river
rock calendar   middle-aged rock   Medicaid rock
single rock   parent rock
shy rock   fixed rock   disagreeing rock
ragged rock   weary rock
resting rock   sweet rock   sensitive rock
rock drift   depraved rock   attentive rock
safe rock   thinking rock
rock bluff   walking rock   original rock
mute rock   meditating rock
rock bible   holy rock   rock world
constant rock   companion rock   clay rock
colored rock   fossiled rock
lonely rock   ready rock   formal rock
lying rock
lying rock
sorry rock to forgiving rock

## Atonement

The pious sober day solemnly descends
on undamaged desert. We rise through bitterbrush
and plumes of native grass, over yucca spines and goathead
prongs, past cracks and dips of swollen dirt. We stumble
once or twice. To the west, the hand of our village spreads;
our hike is slow, our mouths grit and powder
on a mountain cupped in a matrix of rock.

At the peak, we see a wooden cross
clenched in dried ribs of earth. The man who bore
this cross lugged the weight of pardon, mounting it here,
where the shoulder of heat is heaviest.
We are unsettled by this silent disciple, stationed
beneath the fading blue. We imagine the effort,
bent-back and ashamed.

Wind sings in S-curves across the remaining stains
from his cramped hands. We've walked the path
he took to drag the cross along the crest.
Gold lines scorched into the juncture of pine
flash with sunlight: his burden of sorrow unconcealed.
An apron of thin air condemns us.
An anthem of absolution settles like ash.

We almost hear the man's full-voweled confession
and the salvation susurrated by the Valley's old priest
since we've seen this penance, the gravity
of carrying error. The sun continues setting on Tetilla Peak
in rusted particles. Our village lies below
in a filigree of light, and a dried coyote jaw
exposes teeth gnawed by time, its elastic cry expired.

## A Form of Light

Four thousand blossoms
                all yellow
        knit over route 94

Wind
weaves into wheat
        through acres of honey-soaked
                pauses

        The dead rise from curves and dips
of their red pinwheels

I care to be not at the center
but the edges

        in ragged light

                where seeds remove the ground
        and fall erases its rewards

What is gold sugar and crimson
will turn brown

        I know
it is about to happen

        I ask to drink from a white cup
        and hear words
                discuss what they know

        Sun bounces off piñon
to touch my glasses

# How I'd Explain What Kind of Mother She Was

When you ask *was she a good mother*, I am back at our Tudor,
that three story building assuaged and slow in its timbre
of browns, back by the screened-in porch bound in its tangle
of snow boots. I have just slammed the door, wrenching
big sounds from my small alone body. My mother is basting,
as always, on our blue-knotted couch under the stickiest sun.
Blue, with its idle permutations and pace, its remarkable poise.
Shaking off slumber, she twists up her fingers, and rises
into the small port of her life. Though she wants to consider
each tiny battle and blank of my day, I just circle around,
and she watches the curve of each pigtail as I ask to go out,
to jump rope, or maybe shoot baskets right-handed toward
the mouth of the moon. What did she do all those long
afternoons as her children dribbled off on their own, and
the day, half-burnt, toppled out of the sky? Our relationship
was always that haunted, that taut and that still. Eleven years
without has made me agreeable to the needs of my grief,
but my mother-hunger is craving more than the dry taste
of restraint. The smear of what's missing has blacked out
perfection. When I am sick now, her cool hand still brushes
my forehead as the thermometer counts, and even now
I hold the despair as she's pulling it out, shaking it down,
dislodging that four-minute figment of touch, so I'll live
with each uncertain lick of disease or infection. I understand
loss is supposed to get lighter, to fly off to the sky, like Chippy,
our poodle who died and she told me in our kitchen,
all yellow and nervy. Offered the news to my eight-year-old
mind, and the ghost of the dog became distant, a shadow
of flying, cramped up with my tin current of laughter.
Oh, how she hated that matted gray dog —
and every dog, bird and rodent that followed. But now,
when I lift my tortoiseshell cat, spoon my hand on the fur
on the low of her belly, scooping and rubbing, if I didn't
learn this at home, how do I know what tenderness is?
I didn't get death, and she didn't explain it. But on each
*yahrzeit* of her papa, her mouth gathered up like a seam,
and her eyes floated sadly around in their harbor. How sour
we were then, holding our edges apart from her odor
of missing, the flurry of tears that extended like waves.
Shaped into stones in a tall house of stones, we passed our

hard surfaces around. I still see her, evenings, in bed
with the *Times* Dad snagged off the Lexington Ave
#6 train he took north from the office, the paper folded
sideways beside her. As an obsolete moon punctured
a moon-sized space through the window, newsprint
decorated her fingers. How often I sat there, needling
and pricking her patience with all of my questions,
hearing the jitter of fingernail nick at her polish. But
only now do I see the papers as some kind of relief
from the sections of home, how headlines typeset that
morning could forecast her feelings. The merciful comfort
of data, how the black words of the page were her wing
of desire, or the lines of the past, and the red wine
on the nightstand drowned the rapid dispatches of Dad
as he argued her failures and crimes, the obituary of days
always buried in days. Maybe she had no taste for the soup
of her children. When I wakened each night lost in my spit,
in the fable of monsters and witches toppling the masts
of my mind, and wanted someone to carry me back,
to help me across my dark street of danger, past the spears
of myself, past the sails falling forward, I gathered
my pillow and stood in the corner of her room by the door.
*Indulgent*, she said, when I woke her, because I read past
my bedtime, then turned pages of mysteries and thrillers
into my sleep. But she pushed at my father, who left me
his warm-body space in their boat-sized bed, so I climbed in,
floating happily up to their night-grafted peace
as Dad lumbered upstairs to snore with my masses of spiders.
After she died, I figured crosswords to keep busy, dreaming
new grids to fill in. Having a finite series of directions erased
what I couldn't reorganize: our ingenious ways to never say *love*.
But I am being unbalanced. She smiled at everyone. Yes,
I am scarred by her leaving our two-sided existence,
the one where she didn't bake cookies, or add notes
to my lunchbox, but I won't ignore those trips to Manhattan
to see the Diors and snow-studded, Christmas-crazed windows.
And as my father idled the Buick, refusing to release change
to the meters, Mom and I sauntered past the procession
of mannequins whose arms turned out neatly at elbows.
We loved each other in hidden ways amid the folds

and tucks of their remarkable gowns. I wonder sometimes
if I just don't remember the Kool-Aid or kisses, like a sieve
letting go of the sand but keeping the stones. Instead,
I see clearly the moment she stood at the foot of the stairs,
tenaciously pressing the banister, and telling me gravely
how I'd ruined her life and postponed her redemption
when I swiped those three pretty pink panties from that store
in the mall. Her anger was always red first. But how
could she mean that when she showed up at the station
and stayed while my fingerprints were taken, and we went
again to movies and museums? And just now as you're waiting
for me to answer your question, I'm recalling how we drove
to Delaware in a downpour, how Mom in the passenger seat
kept lurching forward as I stuttered and struggled the car
through the nebulous dark. While I worried invisible ghosts
of the road, she gently read me each drop of the rain,
never irritated, never mocking my fear that the dark future
would harm us. We kept skating forward on those four
hinky wheels, both of us trusting the low mist of headlights
hazily lighting the long confused road to the end.

## Counting

One day you will return to catalog my progress in this world.
Two times I will smile

though I may not know you anymore.
Three hours will elapse as we search the earth for comfort.

Four thousand people will cross paths in a city
five times around the globe.

We will drive there to see the marks they leave behind.
We will each bring six dreams, and I will tell you mine first.

You will remind me that almost seven years have passed,
then study me for lines of disbelief.

Eight times I will kiss you and the space you left behind.
Nine times you will bend to stroke my hair

and nine times nine you will cover me with prayers.
On the tenth day, we will balance on our heads, look sideways

into each other's biggest, brownest eyes
as though looking into a mirror of ourselves.

# A Gravitational Lens
*(or How My Mother Returned)*

I stand in a pool of systemic sunshine, watching my mother command her small skiff through molecules of descending heaven. She has never appeared in a green boat before. She rubs wooden oars across the sand: one in, one out. I love her like this. She's beautiful, but faint. I'm surprised that she is an elegant seafarer, but the rabbi remarked on her contradictions and strength at her funeral. Of course, then I wasn't listening. In all these years, she's had time to navigate the engine of death. She tosses a cape over the arch of her back. My mother has dark hair again. She offers a slight smile, which I almost miss. The molten sky floats by. A silken sun settles in my pocket. I watch only the route of my mother. She slicks the boat through dry land, rowing past an irrelevant swell of dust. I've never seen her this forceful. I am enthralled that the desert opens to her. For the first time in a decade, I am calm, waiting out the banner of wind from the west, and looking both ways into a glowing sea of ruffled light, my palms full of broken eyeglasses.

# Three

## Driving South

Drive south down a city on the lip of the Sonoran desert,
an ancient point ravaged with excessive light —

the horizon, a tightrope pulling peak to mountain peak,
a liquid landscape of sky suspended on an upper edge
and the outside singing the hymn of morning.

Drive through a turquoise tunnel, past homeless men
asleep on illiterate stone, disintegrating sand,

drunk, barefoot, unashamed. See Lorca fish for the moon
and Picasso form paint into human rectangles of face.

Hear Neruda's random odes, but know the great gods
are dead, the eternal drawn in cracked lines on paved roads.

Forty miles down, the car peers over a fisted hill;
a valley peels across the dashboard.

Drive, drive on through solemn brush of early day.
Tongue air clotted with dust. Don't tell anyone you're here,
engrossed in chapters of the largest sky.

# A Week in L.A.

### Beverly Hills Boulevard

Sharon Stone has been walking down Beverly Hills Boulevard in a gold halter top for years. She holds a small pebble in each hand. The pebbles have golden hair, like hers. You and I have entered the velvet shape of public experience where people curl up next to each other without touching. They travel in carriages of their slight bodies, stippling eight-inch stilettos on sidewalks. It is any day of the week, our mouths thick with the merciless truth of Splenda.

### Venice Beach

A map on the boardwalk reveals a flat side, where gravity passes through keychains and skate shops. Sun drops like powdered sugar between slats of fence. We walk under umbrellas and visors, past the world's greatest cowboys and Rastas on bikes, through joking and piercings, into the waltz and step of the ocean, into waves that become blue apostrophes, into long omissions of space. The shadows have never been clearer.

### Toward Manhattan Beach

Traffic laps at the road, thirsty for motion. We pass trees made of numbers as we creep toward the delicate brow of horizon. Smog falls in steel clumps. Cars shift through long hours of day. I notice the narrow margin, the crashes arranged on the interstate, the knotting of space. Each evening, we eat the tight sacrifice of tension in six-ounce containers. Flavor disappears. Empty Styrofoam notch and pile in the trunk.

### Beverly Hills Boulevard (2)

A photographer runs backward, his lens opening like a mouth to swallow former people. Everyone is angled, held in the ever-shrinking linen and spandex of self. Sharon Stone is sullen, dragging her pebbles. Sun smacks her forehead. A polite alarm goes off inside her gray-blue eyes, but we cannot hear it. I realize she lives next door to nowhere in a field of plush carpet. Eager flowers loop up off the sidewalk in cowlicks of hope. We hold our bodies erect.

## A Condo on Wilshire

I remember the small gripping muscles of home, its sea green walls and the slow fan brushing warm kisses over my forearms. In a moment of panic, I dial for connection, my voice hazy with privacy, then adjust to the glass panes. I linger in the oblique experience of watching cars dredged in a furry sun, their bodies wiping down the road. What to hope for? The illusion of perspective, each moist soliloquy of light. Wine every night.

## At Gate 2, LAX

The exit door alarm articulates, offering a pompous one-sided scream, a warning sign for the already broken. I want the next transition, the stampede of people toward overhead bins. We've been to the grill, the trattoria, the lounge. Sipped and sucked at ourselves. Time to flutter back from folded dawns and studded examples to the dull hiss of desert. Time to arrive mid-sentence devastated by snow.

## Fixed Gaze of Winter

Winter distends glassy-eyed into spring.
We watch a sun sidle to the next lot,
and hear the sins and habits of baby goats.

Mooning headlights drift
across our dirt road,
interrupting our private behaviors.

We're desperate already — all surface
and chill, afflicted with blood and ice.
Our shadows barely move.

Locked in repeating layers, we hear
the applause of wind repeat as winter hovers
under a parasol of naked olive trees.

We read each paragraph of waiting
on the weather-stained soles of our shoes,
a reflection of all the steps we won't take.

In this season of tumbling texture,
we are entitled
to the thin crust of blue-eyed distance.

And that's all we want
— to look out at the gouged expanse
where ground once lay.

## Knock Knock

I got out the pinking shears and sliced up
today's newspaper. Little airborne triangles of newsprint
fluttered to the floor. Libya became Lib,
Lib became Bill, and I remembered my friend,

and how, when we were kids in 1973,
we belted out the Oreo song.
(Back then, all TV commercials qualified as songs
in my limited musical library.)

But I won't sing it for you now.
There's nothing to sing about.
The news is thick enough that three pages hurt my palm.
The scissor blade dulled.

The flickers all tell knock-knock jokes this time of year,
and another part of the house sinks into a hole.
I pull you outside to see the damage.

We stand in the platter of mulch I tossed down
to cover Elizabeth's double-headed black hollyhock seeds.
*Look down*, I say. *You're stepping on them!*
*They'll never grow now.*

## Rabbits

One Sunday morning I was digging a hole
for a thyme. Warm sun sat on my knees.

I shoved a red-handled trowel to earth, and pressed
with the heel of my hand. The blade squealed

as I poked open a hole filled fine with fur
to a kindle swaddled in twigs

and dry leaves, coated in ground.
The light-bruised hollow was wrong, and no longer

beneath, so I patched the warren
with layers of land, veiled out the light.

Two mornings later (with the mother still AWOL),
David woke early from worry. Pulled on

old jeans. Outside, he gathered the five tender forms
in his gloved palm. They wriggled

and he wrapped them in cloth and put them soft
in a dishpan, green as spring. Light was seeded

with gray. He might have talked to them,
everything he never says

about hunger and need. He held them
under the faucet by the apricot tree,

where nature was climbing the bark
and its branches. He covered them in water

while I slept, consecrated those five alone bodies
in sleep while the warm-flowered dawn

helped me plant dreams. I saw what I saw
through closed eyes as tree shadows fell.

The effort exhausted him,
the moisture poured over those hearts.

# Eyelid and Eyelid of Slumber

*The Time-Out Mystery*

he put his arm out
I sleeping was

in the fire trees
and the teacup of chestnuts

*love* I called him
once or never

in invisible red
minutes

lips
and secret

light:
I did not hear

while I stood
in a ladder of my body

and stayed
lashed to blue

*Sleep Study*

In 2001, I joined a study at a sleep clinic in Albuquerque, looking for an answer to my insomnia. I sat in a bright room with twelve exhausted people for two hours each Wednesday afternoon. Some fell asleep, then woke up. Their eyelids were circles, and the circles showed me that they were constantly moving away from themselves.

The doctor told us to fight our dreams. His philosophy was simple: Ask for exactly what you want. Each session ended with some residue of the experiment on our eyes. At home, I threw away my clock and applied what I learned to the sheets.

The medicine of sleep allowed for one remarkable interaction in color every four days. I always misplaced the reason for my dreams. Before long, I found the silhouettes of my memory in a book, written in someone else's handwriting. Other people turned pages with white gloves.

*Stage 4: REM*

I climbed into the bed. I climbed into a trunk
outfitted with crisp green sheets. The trunk had no lid
and I fell asleep with my arms under me.

We were strolling through the park, my arms crisscrossed
in yours, when I noticed a phone flashing 110 messages.
Numbers ticked away, faster and faster.

Even without answering, I knew it was my father.
He is the only person who would leave so many
messages in my dreams.

I climbed into a forest where I watched a woman in white scrubs
perform surgery. She was relocating a face to a breast.
I climbed to California, to the beach.

Overhead, cedars annotated the sky with their long limbs.
I climbed into a Zen monastery
where I sat very still.

## An Old Story

The moon laughs, but this is an old story,
jam green and fat around the middle,
the burden of proof on one unlucky man
who climbed a tree and touched an apple,
tasted the sugar of distraction. In the beginning,
the man lived in a world without form.

God made the man from dust and thorns.
God gathered particles of heaven and earth
to build a paradise around that man who watched
waters curve into banners and turn ocean.
The man heard sounds he'd never known.
He marveled at the wild beasts.
He lived in the garden with all creeping things
and the fish and fowl. When God gave the man a woman
to play with, the man smelled the woman all over,
and God saw this was good. Man took the woman into him;
he married her. He built a house from wood
he found nearby; he fell asleep in her reliable arms.

Then God gave man another woman.
God was too busy creating light
to pay attention. The man cleaved to the other woman
and her rib bones, the parts lower down that fold and pucker,
and something was severed in his house.
No one talked very loud; there was nothing to say.

God kept working on his world; no time to rest.
He created secrets, then rage and fingernails.
God fermented the plants that grew in the Garden,
and man drank the liquid every day, every night
until strange creatures swam inside the man.

God continued in a bustle of activity. Time was tenuous,
passing — day four, day five. Day six: locks
and cell phones, then God created Xanax, Serax,
Zoloft and Prozac, credit cards and email,
Paxil and headaches, lying and lawyers.
And on the seventh day, God rested.

## That One Night

That one night
the moon turned purple
then faded to persimmon
in a back alley
while they traded rings of cold air.

That one night he was her suitor.
She befriended the goddesses
and warlords of the dark
and took his hand.

The night was filled
with her mother or it was a dusty wind
that she kept grabbing for.

That one night she understood
the chart of elements;
cold was bathed in sustenance,
and stones told stories to inner walls,
crooned again because they needed it.

That one night the moon became full.
The sky stood by, a cloudy tangle,
trickling rich secrets down
in the guise of sweet white
disappearing flakes.

## Desire

She sits inside
something savage,

the sound of the enemy
becoming desire,

memory,
the tongue and groove

furrowed into her marrow.
Hope scatters

everywhere,
her smile flapping about

and she untidy
in her own static.

Love is ash-
tinged, the smoke

easier to watch
when it wraps

around someone else.
Even though

her breath is dressed
in ferocious colors,

the sun hangs casually
above.

## That Unsafe Place

It began with the artichoke green of home,
a note that said *available*, an afterthought,
an older man tasting the bite and breath
of morning — then, a blizzard of skin,
his beard skimming her thighs. She sighed,
cobwebbed with exhaustion, driving dusted
passion through unstable dignity, the dead-
end day on its dead-end knees — and *please,
each night evaporate this flimsy line of freedom.*
She gathered her daggers, the cloak of desire.
He was always inside her building, always
shaping artifice. The jittered fist of her heart
knotted up. It would not be an easy year.
His lickerish last words lingered, though
she kept deleting all the letters, letting them
cool, laying them bare. Why subscribe to
knobby nights, notch each torn-up morning,
and weep once per hour when the entire
framework of her life was set? She owned
no discipline, paced in opposite directions
through pauses and roaring. A person can't
move toward these sorts of worlds without
the blunt end of fear pouring out, without
the wrong kind of bearing, but never mind.
She swallowed the succulent, knowing what
she rendered could ruin her. At long tables,
she sipped her scarlet self and its forbidden
meanings; in random beds, she offered an
inverted axis of reason, pulled her body open,
aimed to free herself. She needed to relax
the bond of bowls and glasses, but wanting
wouldn't leave her. He undid her in a Volvo;
he undid her anyplace. It woke her up,
and for a while she thought she'd walk
into any man, through the unsteady
obstruction of winter, summer, sadness, into
the exegesis of her own ancient story. But
nothing's ever zero option, and everything's
not beautiful. Or safe, or kind, or hopeless.

## No, wait...

Let me try again to explain.

    The story goes backward at one point,
leaving only broken dots of color. She folds the heartache
between pages of a book she doesn't like. Are you in love?

*Yes*, she would've said
        — and *no*. She is bigger now, still tender.

# Confession

I guess everybody needs a place to confess —
for you, my living room where I am sitting, hot,
legs folding and unfolding like a map.

Your voice is gunfire in the distance
but I hear it well. The day discharges
in thin beams of cheer and shafts of sober light.

Two hummingbirds screech outside
the open window, sniping,
beak-sharp into their territory. Neither eats.

You push your hands against your back
and your mind pours out.

You were a doctor and a spy, sharing beers
with a Russian friend, collecting evidence,
the great game of "caring for your country"

but you pressed a hidden button,
and a rift sang in the earth. The ocean opened.

A pawn for a paycheck, you slipped
into a dirty mixture of emotion and distraction,
doing ten years' penance.

Every day you sewed your guilt
to ruined organs, your touch like a filigreed prayer
and the need to heal nearly pulsing.

Sitting here in your used-up self,
you taste the forty-year secret and the sacrament
of hope. This afternoon you ask

if it ever stops, as though I'd know about forgiveness,
as if I don't listen to my own deceits
hovering and humming always in my ears.

# Journey

### 1. Arriving

I have come to Ireland to gather the rivers because I could not sleep
in my bed. Strangers and sorrows, evenings and autumn.

Days stuck in a finite space where all attention moved
repeatedly inward, draining me.

Here is the green side of the world. The river Liffey rolls
through my back pocket and the river Shannon drowses in my shoe.

Sweet the brine, sweet the sky. Sweet even the endless sound
of my father's voice. Sweet the distance from where I live.

Looking down, I see clouds. Cliffs become my marrow,
the ocean, my prophet. I slurp cream soup noon and supper.

### 2. Dublin

The brick city rumbles with commerce and gray water,
each street unsorted into north and south. Crowds move into gaps
and pulse through a rill of fissured language:

words that tickle and stumble, words in brown jackets,
brown shoes, words that hurl and kick, pray and dance.

A beaded raindrop lands on another in a long melody.

I want to read the Book of Kells, turn illuminated pages
of pomegranate and orange nectar pollinated with gold streams
of limned words,
                 but I climb the Trinity stairs
where faint music floats like psalms from a thousand rows
of volumes. The unity of dust and old ink,

almost too much to bear. Books tired, but alert,
murmur endlessly of their matter.

### 3. North to Sligo

We stand at the crust of the water as long letters move
from their reverie to the ragged edge

of Yeats' grave. Sun nibbles through a thick mist.
Innisfree crouches on the shore. I lean in

to Benbulben's shadow. A Celtic cross binds each rime
and arc of wind. The lingering fog rises from an unresolved

sky. Silence swells. Survival is shallow like this.

### 4. A Pint
On a curved street in Carrick-on-Shannon.

On a wood stool near a stranger.

With a pint of muddy beer.

A bowl of roast parsnip soup.

The tide exhaling across the way.

By a silver rail.

By the skirt of the dreary sun.

On the scarf on the scruff of the island.

Everything in this tavern is a chant and a ritual.

We set our conversation on the counter.

Time refuses to continue.

### 5. Lough Derravaragh, County Westmeath
I have become lost in the rustle of trees, the grass carpet,
spill of shadows sheep-stained on dormant hills.

I listen to the courtly skies and my father's epic distractions.
The island opens in a bouquet of rain; bees turn into warriors.

A soft day, the vestige of harvest. The land is a green glissando.
Wind soldiers on, and the sky shakes.

### 6. Warning
Don't walk into a fairy circle.
If you move through fields of Sitka spruce, through bogs,
into an island of oak, ash, hazel and holly,
beware the sweet gospel
of their voices, the stream and giggle of movement.

You won't need a compass to see the signs.
Beware the tiny girl-bodies as they strut,

their doll eyes dancing. Their spirits reside in the heather,
in tiny specks of yellow gorse
in the weak, wet, westernmost world.

If you are tangled in yourself, carry cold iron
and cast your bells on the night wind,
or the changelings will capture you,
flicker and pirouette on your sadness, pinch and pull
until you are sediment in the forest.

### 7. Most Days Only Slubs of Light

A tatted fog drapes the view, the sky nearly erased,
drifting away in gray-green drops. I traveled to forget

and found ordinary days, barefoot and hopeful
as the ones I left behind. Our car rolls through towns
with ruddy names, a confluence of rivers and vowels.

Amber trunks grow slow and straight with verdant tops.
Autumn loops in eighteen strains of green.

I am learning to scavenge the inner corners,
fetch beer and biscuits, see pink in green seas

under pinpoints of light under the chorus of clouds.
A long curve of calm consoles me. What I feared once

has drizzled from my hands. Soon I will return
to scabbed cedars and spiny hopsage, to the tremble

and sigh of stars in the desert,
the bright skin of mornings brewing.

## To Be Still

Sometimes you have to drive
through a river basin and a bracelet of cypress
to find the center of forgetting.

It is practical to be sitting here,
seeing down to acorns,
unknotting into the umbrella of each tree.

The sky has not fallen, not yet.
If you have to move to be still,
be satisfied by this.

Let the world offer the roughed-up edges
of a stacked wall, each stone talking
about what it cannot contain.

Rubbing the day against your small self,
you realize the pitch of water,
the crowning balm of lavender.

The sun settles sideways
on a field of seeded columbine;
the heart of June is the slope of dusk.

Sparrows and finches sing
on their absent-minded journey
past dandelion brush heads.

The red-leafed ash, lobelia and catmint
all gather nearby — in concentration,
not making a sound.

## The Coming Day

I float on a sea of Joni Mitchell songs, hibernate
in the playground she wants to save. My eyes are inside.

The suburbs burst from a small seed in the backyard,

just a murmur now, but in seven years we will be locked in
with something that really happened, a world that germinated

while we loved. The birds will merge with the invisible.
God will move to the outside, forget us and

our five-minute increments of sanity. We are asleep,

touching particles, sowing atoms of air. In the morning,
there are gentle tugs. Flickers impregnate the eaves.

The grasses grow. I hear your heart beat across the down,
feel your eyes burn along my face.

When I am more awake, I sit up, split clementines

into sections, line them up along the bedspread,
count the ripe parcels of the coming day.

# When

When he mentions sacrifice, think a body
    stripped to the waist.

When we talk trust, consider thaw,
    scuffed shoes bending forward.

When you hear "common," think black on white.
    Think black without.

When you discuss "if," draw up the fire.

For vertiginous space, visualize communal passage.
    Open a tin of memory.

When you shiver, you enter the radical center
    — or tangible timidity.

When you see hands, think natural order
    lingering just above the ground.

When you hear a perfect recitation of Beethoven's 5th
    or stand in the storm of Twombly's scribbles,

when you are lost in Breughel's watery green
    or Twain's drawl,

stop the suffering and ask for exactly what you want.
    Pretend your pupils are the reciprocal compass of sight.

Crouch into the smear of a tulip, the tragic palette of time.

When you think minimum output, desire the window.
    Count falcons, focus, release.

# Acknowledgments

*Thank you to the following journals whose editors first accepted these poems for publication, sometimes in slightly different forms.*

"Looking Around These Days" in *The Fox Chase Review*

"November" in *The Spoon River Poetry Review*

"Rail Runner Express Crash on 1-25 South of Santa Fe" in *Untitled Country Review*

"Toward Summer" in *dirtcakes*

"Drama Class, 1989" in *Sin Fronteras*

"Time" in *The Quotable*

"Unpacked" in *Santa Fe Poetry Broadside*

"Girl on a Bus" in *Untitled Country Review*

"And Now You Would" in *Adobe Walls Anthology*

"For Those of You" in *Sin Fronteras*

"Ten Years" in *The Quotable*

"My Grandfather and His Eggs" in *Artistica 'zine*

"Even If" in *J Journal*

"Let Me Live in Your Tolerance" in *The New Verse News*

"Dream Pantoum" in *Two Weeks Anthology*

"In Provincetown" in *Looking Back to Place Anthology*

"What You Might Hear" in *World Literature Today*

"Thelonious Monk On A Subway" in *World Literature Today*

"Value + Pauses" in *Solo Novo Poetry Journal: 122 Days*

"Philadelphia" in *Malpaís Review*

"The *uh-huh* of Desire" in *Halfway Down the Stairs*

"Clarity" in *The Journal of Compressed Creative Arts*

"Out walking" in *Adobe Walls Anthology*

"The Dailiness" in *Untitled Country Review*

"A Colloquy on Water" in *Manorborn Anthology*

"When You Leave, Reiterate the Alarm" in *The New Verse News*

"Everything Human" in *Adobe Walls Anthology*

"At Echo Canyon" in *Untitled Country Review*

"Atonement" (as "Brother to Brother") in *Cæsura*

"A Form of Light" in *Untitled Country Review*

"How I'd Explain What Kind of Mother She Was" in *J Journal*

"Counting" in *Accolades* chapbook, SFCC Student Writing Competition

"A Gravitational Lens" in *you are here*

"A Week in L.A." in *Solo Novo Poetry Journal: 122 Days*

"Driving South" in *Sin Fronteras*
"Fixed Gaze of Winter" in *Adobe Walls Anthology*
"Knock Knock" in *The New Verse News*
"Rabbits" in *Sin Fronteras*
"Eyelid and Eyelid of Slumber" in *Malpaís Review*
"An Old Story" in *Poetica*
"That One Night" in *Santa Fe Literary Review*
"Desire" in *Yemassee*
"That Unsafe Place" in *you are here*
"No, wait..." in *Santa Fe Literary Review*
"Confession" in *J Journal*
"Journey" in *you are here*
"To Be Still" in *New Mexico Poetry Review*
"The Coming Day" in *The Kerf*
"When" in *Adobe Walls Anthology*

"A Colloquy on Water" was also published in *How to....Multiple Perspectives on Creating a Garden, a Life, Relationships and Community* (Old School Books). Lauren also read this poem in the PBS documentary film "Earth Chronicles Project: New Mexico."

"Let Me Live in Your Tolerance" was also included in *The Más Tequila Review*.

"November," "Unpacked," "Let Me Live in Your Tolerance," "At Echo Canyon," "My Grandfather and His Eggs" and "The *uh-huh* of Desire" were reprinted in the Spring 2013 issue of *Malpaís Review*. Thank you to Margaret Randall for the interview that accompanied the poems.

"Unpacked" was also included in *Cradle Songs: An Anthology on Motherhood* (Quill & Parchment).

An audio version of "Girl on a Bus" was included in *Red Lion Square*.

"Eyelid and Eyelid of Slumber" takes its title from a line in "Moonrise" by Gerard Manley Hopkins.

## About the Author

Lauren Camp is an artist and educator, working in the confluence of visual, musical and literary worlds.

She produces and hosts "Audio Saucepan," a global music/poetry program on Santa Fe Public Radio. She also writes the poetry blog *Which Silk Shirt*, and constructs the web installation *Notes to Cecil*. Her poems have appeared in *J Journal*, *Linebreak*, *Beloit Poetry Journal*, *World Literature Today* and other publications. Lauren has received residencies from the Gaea Foundation and the Mabel Dodge Luhan House. She holds degrees from Cornell University and Emerson College. Her first book, *This Business of Wisdom*, was published in 2010.

Lauren is also an acclaimed visual artist. Her solo exhibit, "The Fabric of Jazz," traveled to museums in ten U.S. cities. Other work has been showcased in major publications and exhibited on movie sets, in cultural centers, museums and U.S. embassies.

She lives in a small farming village in northern New Mexico.

www.laurencamp.com